DISTANT ECHOES

A Gathering of Queer Poems

DISTANT ECHOES

A Gathering of Queer Poems

MILES CIGOLLE

SUNSTONE
PRESS

SANTA FE

Sunstone books may be purchased for educational, business, or sales promotional use.
For information please write: Special Markets Department, Sunstone Press,
P.O. Box 2321, Santa Fe, New Mexico 87504-2321.
Printed on acid-free paper
∞
eBook: 978-1-61139-755-0

Library of Congress Cataloging-in-Publication Data

Names: Cigolle, Miles, author.
Title: Distant echoes : a gathering of queer poems / Miles Cigolle.
Description: Santa Fe : Sunstone Press, 2024. | Summary: "In this memoir of
 queer poems, the author feels blessed with generous love for himself and
 his brothers"-- Provided by publisher.
Identifiers: LCCN 2024037992 | ISBN 9781632936844 (paperback ; acid-free
 paper) | ISBN 9781611397550 (epub)
Subjects: LCGFT: Queer poetry.
Classification: LCC PS3603.I354 D57 2024 | DDC 811/.6--dc23/eng/20240819
LC record available at https://lccn.loc.gov/2024037992

WWW.SUNSTONEPRESS.COM
SUNSTONE PRESS / POST OFFICE BOX 2321 / SANTA FE, NM 87504-2321 /USA
(505) 988-4418

for
Jim Bruce
in loving memory

Contents

Preface

*T*his book of queer poems explores the delicate art of wordsmithing. The sound of each word is special, creating personality and feeling. Pacing and rhythm give it life. Rhyme can make us chuckle or drive us completely mad. Alliteration may make us smile; a double meaning can make us cry. It's like an elaborate house of cards, where each word impacts the others, where the total is always greater than the fragment, like in an opera by Mozart.

Good poetry gets inside our heads. It won't let us sleep at night. It comes back in the shower or while we're making love. It's one of life's greatest pleasures, up there with kittens and mistletoe. A simple poem of Japanese haiku with just three lines can touch us to our core.

The fifty-one poems in Distant Echoes span two distinct styles. The first half are primarily free verse in conversational delivery focusing primarily on themes of queer sex, love, fitting in and queer dreams. The poems are loose, and equally embrace humor and queer eroticism. The second half are highly structured poems generated by the twenty-six letters of the English alphabet. They are more compact, consisting of double-rhyme four-line poems of six stanzas each. Despite the straight jacket on these small poems, they are as inventive as their free-verse free-love brothers and sisters. All the poems beg to be read out aloud. If you find a line funny, please feel free to roll on the floor. Poetry should make us happy and sad at the same time. Never read poetry while driving or having sex. Reading poems alone or with a dearest beloved is the closest thing to finding heaven on earth.

1 ~ A Father's Blessing

The boy had an arm around each dog,
he was no bigger than either.
Two Labradors, a vanilla and a chocolate,
they occupied more than half of the counter.

The waiter seemed in the least bit concerned,
his new guests were a welcome change.
A ragamuffin as cute as this,
was certainly more than an even exchange.

The lad was absolutely adorable,
his blond straw hair pulled in every direction.
He couldn't have been much older than the beasts,
counting canine years upon reflection.

The chocolate was on a leash,
held by the boy's Italian father.
The blond belonged to an elegant lady,
who was assured it would be no bother.

The chocolate was clearly his best friend,
the vanilla was his newest buddy.
Competing equally for the boy's affection,
they were both just a little bit muddy.

The father was busy with his espresso,
as was the lady gossiping with a local nun.
Both were content to leave the boy in charge,
who was clearly having serious fun.

In a most public display of affection,
the father turned to whisper a prayer.
He first stopped to plant a kiss,
on his son's mop of golden hair.

The boy angel took it all in stride,
the dog's unfiltered affection,
the smiles from the café patrons,
his father's complete adoration.

As they turned to leave the cafe,
onto the deserted flight of steps.
The boy angel took the leash in his hand,
following closely in his father's footsteps.

2 ~ Cis Male

I knew I had a penis,
I identified as male.
Even as a baby,
people were startled by the size.
My penis had distinction,
it stood out in a crowd.

I loved my male body,
so full of erotic magic.
Even as a baby boy,
I paid it full attention.
Peeing was so thrilling,
just to hold it in my hand.

Peeing outdoors was tremendous,
a great source of happiness.
Playing tag on the trellis,
with my naked naughty pals.
I proudly held my penis high,
on display for all to see.

At five I discovered the local pool club,
with its showers for boys and men.
My head felt warm and fuzzy,
surrounded by so much flesh.
They were beautiful to look at,
wearing mounds of soapy suds.

Swollen cocks and dangling balls,
I'd rarely seen these things before.
I thought they were magnificent,
one day I'd look the same.
That day came six years later,
when I had my first wet dream.

After that day I jerked off every night,
I loved to stroke my rod.
The tip felt just amazing,
I shared it with my buddies.
We'd shoot our wads of creamy cum,
airborne across the meadow.

Ms. Ewing was my piano teacher,
I was only seven years old.
She had a baby grand,
I could barely reach the pedals.

The piano filled up her living room,
it was on a raised platform.
The carpet was papal purple,
I told her I loved the color.

I played Chopin for beginners,
nocturns, preludes and waltzes.
Plus a little bit of Beethoven,
along with some Broadway tunes.

The lessons were always too short,
I never wanted to go home.
Ms. Ewing always gave me a hug,
I loved her French perfume.

At my first recital, I chose a piece by Chopin,
I was terribly nervous.
Terry was in the audience,
I had dressed up with a bowtie.

I panicked and froze on stage,
I was so embarrassed.
Terry took me for an ice cream,
she never said a word.

A year later Van Cliburn came to town,
I was so excited, Van was my hero.
Terry got us a pair of tickets,
just the two of us, a special treat.

Van was a tall and lanky Texan,
with the world's most beautiful smile.
His fingers were extremely long,
his hair was thick and curly.

I had a total crush on Van,
I felt dizzy when he walked on stage.
He played Rachmaninoff with feeling,
my face was covered with tears.

After the final encore, I went a little crazy,
I begged Terry to take me backstage.
I was extremely lucky,
I found Van in a corridor all alone.

I hugged him like a father,
I told Van that I loved him.
He was just so super nice,
Van rubbed me on my head.

He asked me what was my favorite piece,
I told Van there was no contest.
"I love when you play Chopin Nocturnes.
They always make me cry."

4 ~ Happiness

A young boy's first real treasure,
my first source of true happiness.
The soft knit rubber pouch,
the 3-inch elastic waistband,
the pair of 1-inch leg straps
that caressed my virgin butt cheeks.

My first pair were Bauer and Black,
in the orange and black box.
"Youth Supporter," pure perfection,
I loved the smell so deeply erotic.
Just putting them on,
made a boy's head spin.

I kept it in the back drawer,
my most private guarded secret.
Only to play with,
when the house was good and empty.
Preening at the full-length mirror,
pleased with the new profile.

The mesh rubbery pouch,
kisses my boy's soft penis.
Expands as it slowly stiffens,
then tightens against my first full erection.
I can feel the wet oily tip,
soaking through the soft spongy pouch.

Most gay guys love their jockstrap,
they wear it when they're out cruisin'.
Nothing is sexier than a BIKE,
bulging through a button fly.
My cock is always safe,
inside the spongy pouch.

It brings me good luck,
when I need it the most.
Like in a crowded backroom,
on Saturday night at The Stud.
The pouch always gets its due attention,
for the blowjobs of my dreams.

I prefer the raunchy old ones,
my vintage Bauer and Black.
My childhood favorite,

still in the back of the drawer.
Now it's torn and a little faded,
the elastic band is starting to go.

But I still like to use it,
sometimes I sleep with it in the nude.
It takes me back to childhood,
to rock-hard erections so fine.
I cherish my Bauer and Black,
it's worth its weight in gold.

5 ~ Coach

No backyard catch with Dad, Edward wasn't present.
Just as well really, I couldn't throw the ball.
Dad worked long hours at Well's Market,
Sundays we all went to Mass.
Then Dad drove us to the airport,
where we watched the planes take off.

Coach Hanson wasn't like the others,
he wore an ironed dress shirt.
His chinos were nice and clean,
plus, he treated me so kindly.
He knew I was picked last,
so he made sure I went first.

Coach Hanson knew I dreaded sports.
"You know Miles, I have an idea.
You have the longest legs in class.
You should be a runner."
That was really something, it was really special,
it was about freedom; I ran just like the wind.

7th grade at Jefferson we had Sex Education,
Coach Hanson was the teacher. I was all excited.
He put up posters of the human sex organs,
I dared not peek at the female.
But I really liked the other,
I knew it looked just like me.

I studied the diagram closely,
it made me think of the pool club.
Men's cocks hanging free,
water running down the shaft.
A silvery stream across the tip,
the tip guys liked to play with.

The last day of Sex Ed, Coach was at his best,
he covered the anatomy of the sex organs.
He gave us proper names; he treated us like adults.
He explained the beautiful ridge at the top,
and the special shaped tip of the frenulum.
He told us they were divine, the source of male pleasure.

6 ~ Mama's Boy

He's the twinkle in his mother's eye, her pride and joy, her little man,
definitely a mama's boy, mama's helper by her side.
Looking for her missing love underneath her kitchen apron,
snuggling up beside her, in the giant bed upstairs.
Mama's sweetie pie, her darling baby cakes,
her keeper of their secrets, of all things large and small.

When did small-fry become a youngster, a handsome fare-thee-well?
On the playground they call him Kid, he's no longer Tadpole.
He's a young man, an adolescent, somehow different,
there's something new between his legs, a first inkling of manhood.
But he's still a mama's boy, her schoolboy with the golden curls,
he's still the one with rosy cheeks, who gossips at her table.

When did he become a young man? What happened to the boy?
Was it at his wet dream, when his hardon first arrived?
That's when he discovered sex, the thrill of jerking off,
stroking cock into the night, shooting cum into the air.
Now he's just the "handsome guy." No more her closest friend.
No more happy cuddling in the giant bed upstairs.

When did he become a cock-tease, showing off the goods?
The self-conscious hunk, posing nude before the mirror?
A Peter Fonda, a James Dean, always hiding his dark secrets,
pics of well-hung dudes and black guys dressing up in leather.
Masturbating day and night, in any kind of weather,
all the while missing mama's laughter round her kitchen table.

The Master steps out in the daylight, a stud dressed in black leather.
Terry can only speculate. "What's happened to my Tadpole?"
Is he a go-go boy, a tearoom queen, a drugged disco dancer?
I conceal my amyl nitrate, I lock my hidden box of sex toys.
No Ma, I'm still your darling angel, the one who never fails you,
the one who shows up Xmas, with your favorite French cologne.

Decades later I've slowly mellowed, I'm seated at the table.
I'm the classy uncle, the father figure, the ever-faithful son.
Respectable, revered, attending family functions.
I do the gym, I wear my suit, I smile in family photos.
I'm content to be remembered as mama's little helper,
the one who keeps her secrets safe, buried and out of trouble.

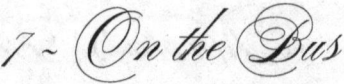

Tim thought he liked girls,
they were sure interested in him.
They always tried to kiss him,
to get inside his pants.

Tim went to school dances,
always prim and proper.
Dancing at a safe distance,
never really touching.

Sure, it was exciting,
or so Tim told himself.
Mother was so pleased,
Tim finally had a girlfriend.

Not so fast, don't draw conclusions,
beware the lie that stifles love.
Tim had a secret lover,
hidden in the shadows.

John was three years older,
a Junior in High School.
He met Tim on a school bus trip,
to the New York World's Fair.

They French kissed in the dark,
in the back of a Greyhound bus.
Their heads were warm and fuzzy,
their cocks were more than eager.

John showed Tim how to make love,
how to give his lover pleasure.
That night changed Tim forever,
he became a queer for life.

That was actually fine,
except it was a secret.
Finally, Tim saw himself clearly,
for the first time in his life.

Years later after college,
Tim ran into John in New York City.
John was a lawyer, married with a little girl,
living the American dream.

Their lives had grown apart,
their paths had separated forever.
Their night of bliss on the bus,
suddenly resurfaced from the past.

John started crying,
the past overwhelmed him.
He hugged Tim for safety,
without saying a single word.

Tim spoke up clearly, "There John buddy,
just remember, I'll always love you.
We will always be together in the dark,
in the back of a Greyhound bus."

8 ~ Dawn

The #1, that's my ticket,
I'm still the anxious tourist.
Emerging from the IRT,
I'm at Sheridan Square.
My heart is pounding, my palms are wet,
my teeth are chattering loudly.

Are all these hot men faggots?
Is he a real street hustler?
I am walking west with them,
these men will be my brothers.
I pass an angel, I pass the devil,
God has forsaken me, left me with no answer.

Christopher Street at midnight,
Faggot City, three blocks to the Hudson.
Standing at the threshold,
at the river's edge.
I'm alone in darkness,
snow will fall before night passes.

The solid white door beckons,
Christopher Street Bookshop.
That is an euphemism,
this is not a bookshop.
This is a sex den, a backroom,
this is my final destination.

This is the moment,
do I have the courage?
I'm jumping off a cliff,
the door is heavy.
My head is numb,
amyl nitrite soothes my nerves.

A Master in black leather,
a nod, a silent welcome.
Black dildos in glass cases,
guys fucking on the screen.
The turnstile to the backroom,
its mechanical clicking sound.

Once inside the sex den,
my hardon feels enormous.
Guys hover in the darkness,
hands rip open my denim fly.

A large hand is on my buttocks,
he's already sucking cock.

Moustache in my fingers,
thick hairs with warm saliva.
My hardon down his throat,
he transports us to heaven.
Midwife to God himself,
my Stud ushers in the dawn.

It's a gay man's favorite topic of conversation,
it's too small, it's too big. It's not thick enough.
It's not as if we order from a Sear's catalogue,
we get what God gives us.
But honestly, they're all really great,
tucked inside a dirty old jockstrap.

The men's showers at the pool club told the whole story,
boys had puny dicks, with very little meat.
Young guys in their twenties, now they had real beauties,
long and thick, gorgeous, I was really jealous.
I assumed the large black stud was an African Prince,
he took the prize for the biggest dick of all.

This was all important, it made a huge difference,
I measured it, it clocked in at six and a half.
I'd tell guys it was seven hard, everybody fibs a little,
I read somewhere, that's on the high side of average.
Porn stars measure seven plus, Black dudes go up to nine,
imagine what that's like, it must be a handful.

Size really makes a difference, but it's not the whole story,
you have to take a look at the total package.
Compare the cock head, to the shaft, to the balls,
then there's the question of beauty, just look at Michelangelo.
His David has a tiny dick, he left the details up to us,
plus David has a bubble butt that grabs our full attention.

I guess it's pretty obvious, I'm a real size queen,
I'm really into the details, I just pay full attention.
You can tell with skinny jeans, especially in the crotch,
the way the fabric pulls around a swollen cock.
Hardons always show, that's what people really notice,
so if you have it, you probably should flaunt it.

I was in the backroom at The International Stud,
a guy in black leather, grabbed my red-hot boner.
He started blowing me, like a real pro,
then he stopped, and looked up smiling.
"God, you have a gorgeous cock."
At that very moment, it all belonged to him.

10 ~ Cabin Boy

The kid was my obsession,
it was pure lust, plain and simple.
The encounters were always brief,
I'd only see him on the Pines ferry.
He was the cabin boy,
surely just a ripe teenager.

Assigned to the open upper deck,
where the ferry pilot sits in his glass enclosure.
I'm not sure what his real duties were,
I guess mostly helping out with the nylon ropes.
I'd see him standing outside the cabin door,
posing in the sunlight.

Not even twelve feet in front of me,
both hands tucked in his front jean pockets.
The way street hustlers pose,
while waiting for their next customer.
Yep, that was the look,
a ready-to-trot street hustler.

I'd always make sure I was seated,
in the front row facing him squarely.
Only a single chain-link swag,
kept me at a safe distance.
He enjoyed playing the cock-tease,
squeezing himself out in the open.

He always wore the same dirty blue jeans,
which showcased a basket of cock.
He'd turn away to show me his buttocks,
Of course, there was no belt.
The pull-over sweat shirt was always zipped open,
it fit snug over his muscular arms.

He had studied his casual look,
from the pages of GQ and Drummer.
I noticed he never wore sunglasses,
despite the intense blinding sun.
Perhaps he sensed they would detract,
from his sweet boyish baby face.

I would wonder what his story was,
he never spoke or smiled.
But then neither did I,

he certainly looked awfully gay.
Was this a Sayville kid's summer job?
Or was he a young gay hustler?

Looking for a rich sugar daddy,
out for a nice piece of ass?
But I always wished him well,
he was gorgeous to lust over.
But he deserved so much more,
he deserved love, most faithful and true.

The Goldberg Variations,
BWV 988, were first published in 1741.
Johann Sebastian Bach,
a musical composition for keyboard.

Consisting of an aria,
and a set of thirty variations.
Named for Johann Gottlieb Goldberg,
the man who first performed it.

A masterpiece without a doubt,
not meant for mere beginners.
Eighty minutes long,
if you think you can survive it.

It's mostly in G major,
starting with an aria so simple.
Glenn Gould's interpretation,
set the world's lofty standard.

"Sex with the Goldberg"
the ad in Grindr was so explicit.
He wore a black leather tuxedo,
while posing in a jockstrap at his baby grand.

He answered the door in his costume,
Glenn was playing in the background.
The baby grand was in the corner,
with the bust of the great Master.

He slapped me with his paddle,
'til my cheeks were rosy red.
He raped me before I knew it,
his cock shoved down my throat.

He parked me in his leather sling,
as the famous aria begins.
He fucked me hard with his boner,
keeping time to Bach's staccato.

Bach's music overwhelmed us,
it was passionate and raw.
Brimming with invention,
transcendent at its core.

With each variation,
we explored our bodies deeper.
Our mouths with their slippery tongues,
our butts with their tender anus.

Thirty variations,
thirty ways of loving.
Rubbing kissing, licking sucking,
biting slapping, rimming fucking.

Queer sex and the Goldberg,
perfect compliments to each other.
Encores of glistening cum,
cascades of shimmering notes.

A faceless tall young Lad,
poses in my doorway.
His white arms stretched up high,
above his head of golden curls.

His luscious white rump is round,
plump like that of Botticelli.
He rubs it with a free hand,
knowing he drives me crazy.

His butt crack is so alluring,
so deep and so inviting.
The cheeks so soft and full,
they make my mouth go dry.

The Lad stares straight ahead,
fully aware he's so hypnotic.
My gaze remains unbroken,
I have nowhere else to go.

I slap his pale cheeks firmly,
they turn from pink to red.
The sound is loud and sharp,
intoxicating inside my head.

I use my bare raw hands,
as he stays in deep repose.
He turns slightly to give approval,
the Lad clearly desires more.

Who is this faceless angel?
My question goes unanswered.
I can only see his buttocks,
a hint of his blond hair.

I finger his deep butt crack,
I rim his silky anus.
He presses back for more,
as we feed each other's lust.

So I fuck him in the doorway,
as he stands with arms raised tall.
My cock is deep inside him,
spilling forth a father's seed.

He remains my faceless angel,
as he turns to walk away.
His rump will always haunt me,
he's the lover I've always craved.

13 ~ *Hustler*

They call him a street hustler,
to me he is a Saint.
Glen hangs out in a doorway,
a Christopher Street fixture.
Beautiful to look at,
My secret dream lover.

I'd gladly take care of Glen,
to massage his beautiful backside.
I'd kiss his fleshy buttocks,
pull open the denim fly.
Glen is extra generous with me,
he knows I just adore him.

He lets me unbutton his cowboy shirt,
to pet his gorgeous six-pack.
I always show him my respect,
after all, he is a legend.
Moguls pay in the high three figures,
just to love him for an hour.

Glen is from Silver Springs, Colorado,
he dreams of open skies.
He still wears the boots and bandana,
to prove he is a cowboy.
He's more at home riding horseback,
than fucking bareback in the porno.

He lets me buy him dinner,
as long as there's no red meat.
He keeps himself tight and trim,
he never touches ice cream.
His butt fills out Levi's nicely,
guys pay double just to fuck him.

He's strictly a free weights guy,
with muscles on top of muscles.
He pushes himself for hours,
with solo workouts at the Chelsea.
Afterwards he hits the steam room,
he even lets black guys blow him.

Glen always greets me with a hug,
he always makes me smile.
He even lets me sleep over,

when business takes a downturn.
I treat Glen to dinner on Mondays,
Glen always orders salmon.

Glen has his future planned out,
he'll say goodbye to hustling.
He's headed to Tumbling River Ranch,
home to horses that need tending.
He'll sleep out under the stars,
dreaming of queens in New York City.

14 ~ The A Team

Bruce Weber's men are cloaked in sex,
always proud to be so butch.
Their fleshy cocks, their beefy butts,
they're all USDA Prime.
American cocks, American butts,
just like a wild American stallion.

Bruce's Men have glamorous smiles,
with picture perfect white teeth.
They steal our love in a heartbeat,
we adore them from across the room.
They're always in monogamous pairs,
on the lookout for a kinky threesome.

Bruce's Men have long thick hair,
the top is sun-bleached like a surfer.
It's never tightly cropped,
it smells salty of the ocean.
They keep it mussed and wind-swept,
as if they've been in the beach buggy.

He strolls the beach in the nude,
looking for his morning hookup.
His stiff cock is dripping wet,
the proud head is slick and oily.
A pretty butt-boy in the dunes,
will be his willing fuck mate.

Bruce's Men stand tall and proud,
their backsides are so erotic.
Young athletes in their prime,
showing off their pale ripe butts.
Two gorgeous smooth pink melons,
the deep crack hot to fuck.

Does glamor detract from their beauty?
Must its cheap artifice offend?
I still study them in complete adoration,
I concede my blind admiration.
Those sun-drenched cocky beauties,
those pagan self-absorbed Gods.

15 ~ Colosseum

It dates back to Emperor Titus,
maybe even further.
The greatest monument of all time,
it's the Roman Colosseum.

Every night after midnight,
it undergoes a transformation.
Roman studs come back for more,
eager to join in the nightly orgy.

Some show up in chariots,
others appear on horseback.
A gladiator strolls by naked,
Nero arrives bareback on a lion.

Roman cocks are on display,
extra thick, long and meaty.
Guys are getting blown,
before the night gets started.

Circle jerks under the vaults,
Cock sucking in the moonlight.
Marcus Aurelius in his golden sling,
waiting to be fist-fucked.

The show goes on all night,
even slaves enjoy their moment.
Young boys are in demand,
butt-fucking is most common.

Hadrian and Antinous make an appearance,
dressed head to toe in leather.
The emperor rims his butt boy,
then he fucks him in the stable.

By the time pre-dawn arrives,
the floor is strewn with bodies.
Guys passed out in darkened corners,
dreaming of last night's lovers.

The call of seagulls is deafening,
the sky overhead is black.
The birds have gone completely mad,
feasting on pools of Roman semen.

Time to hit the Baths of Caracalla,
the body needs a rinsing.
The cocks could use a rest,
before the games get started.

Centuries later, it still goes on and on,
lines form outside the Colosseum.
You can feel the sexual heat,
their balls are getting heavy.

The cycle never ends,
the fucking goes on forever.
Emperor Titus is still revered,
his golden cock is still an idol.

16 ~ *That Boy*

First and foremost, I work my own sidewalk, strictly empty in the daytime.
Nighttime is too rough, too many wackos. I prefer drive-by customers.
Uniformed chauffeurs in exotic foreign cars like a Bentley or a Rolls.
I favor denim over leather, old and raunchy. Show them my jockstrap.
No belt. No shirt. Skin-tight 501s. I have to feel like I'm poured into them.
A big crotch is essential. It can't be overstated. It's alright if it looks unreal.

An old lamp post works the best for posing. Open visibility all around.
One knee raised with the legs parted. Make sure you're facing traffic.
I prefer old sneakers with no color. Crotch visibility is essential.
You want them to see the bulging cock. Go ahead, squeeze it, make him wet.
That's what they came for. Let them salivate, let their imagination run wild.
Play it raunchy. Show him your six-pack, the top of your pubic hair.

As I step to the curb I see the reflection of my basket in the tinted window.
Here's when I play with myself a bit. Massage it. Adjust the position.
The chauffeur rolls down the back window. I approach slowly with a smile.
I make sure he has a clear sight line to my crotch. I slowly pull out my dick.
I fondle the shaft. "So, you want some of this? It's gonna cost you."
They always look so grateful, that I'm even here at all.

Nodding, the chauffeur exits to open the passenger door.
The car interior is dark with a comfy bed for two inside.
"Please enter Sir. This is James. He has long admired your beauty."
Now I am curious. I lean into the limo. James and I make eye contact.
He could be my father, an impeccably dressed businessman.
"Go ahead James. You want it right? It's all yours. Take it in your mouth."

"I know you. You're Miles. I've seen you in Hellfire fucking boys.
Now it's time to fuck a real man. Fill me with your jissom. Give me life."
James grabs me by the crotch, pulling me into the limo onto the bed.
The chauffeur pulls away. James offers amyl nitrate and takes a hit himself.
He rips open my button-fly, swallowing the shaft whole tip to base,
taking it deep in the throat. James is rough and demanding. He wants it all.

James's passion has lit my fire, I'm rock solid, red-hot to trot.
"I'll show you what the boys at Hellfire missed. I'm gonna rape your pretty butt.
Are you ready to be fucked man? Are you ready for my hardon up your tight ass?"
I start weeping. I can't continue. I stop. I caress James. He's my father, my elder.
"Forgive me James. Let me hold your head. Let me show you my respect.
Forgive me father. I can do better. Please forgive me."

Party Boys. It was a long, cold winter,
the boys arrived in the nick of time.
I'd been looking forward to their faces,
their cute butts in skimpy cut-offs.
They're busy catching up on gossip,
checking out the competition.

Party Boys. I study each of them, their casual demeanor,
their extravagant youth, their guilt the morning after.
They flaunt their beauty like drugstore cowboys,
knowing the stage belongs to them.
They strut around like peacocks,
showing off their many feathers.

Party Boys. I envy them, their pretty butts,
their ample cocks, my party days are over.
I recall the thrill of my first Speedos,
my erection showing through.
I'd jerk-off in the outdoor shower,
a butterfly in heat.

Party Boys. I was a poor example,
I never really played their game.
My interest was mostly sex,
not the latest disco craze.
You'd more likely find me sucking cock,
not line dancing in the Pines Pavilion.

Party Boys. "Headed to the Rack?"
"Yes, it's my first time."
"Let me show you the ropes Kid,
don't worry, I won't touch you."
"Could we just walk along the ocean?"
"Sure, the night belongs to you."

Party Boys. We're all in this together,
so tired of loneliness.
Party boys who mix disco and drugs,
or guys like me into raunchy sex.
Both trying to fit into our tribe,
bonding with our sexy brothers.

Angel was just too beautiful.
How could he be anything else?
He was born to be a porn star,
arriving buck naked in his crib.
Lying on his tummy,
showing off his pretty butt.

You really needed to see it,
your imagination wouldn't do.
By the time he was in grade school,
it seemed like everybody knew.
Boys lined up in the showers,
just to touch his pretty dick.

Back then it wasn't massive,
just perfect in every way.
His mother spoiled him rotten,
with a wardrobe fit for a prince.
His salon haircuts alone,
cost a hundred fifty dollars.

He disappeared in high school,
fleeing Tulsa on a bus.
He ended up in West Hollywood,
turning strangers on the strip.
A porn producer saved him,
put him on the silver screen.

He appeared opposite famous beefcakes,
who weren't allowed to touch him.
His contract made it clear,
his cock was to be hidden.
His bubble butt was world famous,
seen on racy Hallmark cards.

He retired at age twenty-five,
doing the TV talk-show circuit.
Sashaying across the big stage,
showing off his stunning butt.
He passed away at thirty,
buried between his Mama and Baby P.

19 ~ A Saint

It's not easy being a saint,
just look at Saint Sebastian.
He was the sweetest guy in town,
good looking, big boner, beautiful butt.
So what did they do?
They shot him full of arrows.

I took good care of Sebastian,
I stopped the damn bleeding.
I shared my bed with him,
I coaxed him back to health.
He slept for over a week,
he healed nicely without any scars.

He woke with a giant erection,
his pre-cum was really sweet.
He asked me to jerk him off,
I blew him nice and easy instead.
His cock was tall and massive, the ridge was crisp and hard.
I licked it like an ice cream cone, it tasted just as fine.

He tended the garden in the nude,
brown rabbits and ducks at his feet.
He sang to the birds and they sang back,
taking shade beneath the old olive tree.
We made slow love in the moonlight,
sharing cock in the fish-net hammock.

I rubbed oil all over his body,
massaging his gorgeous backside.
He asked me to rim his butt-crack,
then slap his butt-cheeks hard.
I told him I'd gladly oblige him,
if he did the same for me.

We both knew our time was over,
I wept in his arms like a baby.
He showered me with his wet kisses,
we shared sweet figs at my table.
Parting at dawn with an embrace,
Sweet Sebastian slipped out of my arms.

He should have, if he could have, but he didn't.
It was too much to ask. After all she said, there's no point.
I really think he was such a lovely person, just a lovely person.
He somehow always got the short end of the stick.
I think it's a crying shame. He got what he had coming to him.
That's for sure. In my book, he was just a fuckin' loser.

Well doesn't that just take the cake? I'm totally flabbergasted.
I wasn't raised like that. He should have known better.
Once a faggot, always a faggot. I told you he was no good.
Now what, you fuckin' moron? You had to go open your big mouth.
I'll keep the back door open. No one has to know.
I'll turn off the porch lights. It will be our little secret.

Fuck you! I'm going. Don't you dare bring it up again.
I could take it or leave it. But now that you ask me, I'll just leave it.
He's the sweetest boy you'll ever meet. But does he put out?
Can I count on him when I really need him?
I'd expect something very special in return.
God, he's gorgeous. How long is his dick? Is he uncut?

I always come here once a year. I hardly knew the guy.
But Abbey always loved him. So I make the trip for Abbey.
It never should have happened. I told him that I loved him.
He brought it on himself. I don't care if everybody knows.
They sure look like brothers. Now that I see them naked, I'd agree.
They had nice dicks too, must be over 7 inches. I'd have taken either.

What was he thinking? He's such a dizzy queen.
I don't know why we come here year after year. It's so overrated.
And expensive. But you're right, the men are something special.
Remember to send Eugene a thank you note. But wasn't it so tacky?
Well, it certainly was triple X, but in the end I really enjoyed it.
I thought it was a first-class act, just waiting for an encore.

In a year, he won't even remember Tom's name.
He has to go through the experience, to grow as a gay man.
But it's still heartbreaking to watch him suffer so,
I was just like him at that age. If anything I was worse.
Remember Allen? He told me he'd always loved me as a father.
I hugged him crying. I told him he was the son I never had.

21 ~ Longing and Belonging

Two wheels and open roads,
It's all about freedom.
How would I know? I don't own a motorcycle.
I've only ridden one once.
Riding on back behind Jed,
it was the high point of existence.

Two wheels and open roads,
it was all about sex and freedom.
The uniform is half the attraction,
the leather cap and gloves, the tight-fitting leather jacket.
The uniform of a rebel,
of a well-lubed sex machine.

My arms tight around Jed's torso,
my hand inside his jacket.
I press myself against him,
Denim crotch to leather chaps.
I feel an erotic connection,
my cock's already hard.

That whole Beat Generation,
weren't they all Harley boys?
Tiny spiral notebooks,
tucked safe inside their jackets.
Just in case their gay muse,
whispers inspiration.

An exclusive brotherhood,
men bonding with each other.
Hidden pull offs just for making love,
guys get horny on the road.
They'll need some extra lubrication,
when doing it on the Harley.

Two wheels and open roads,
It's all about sex and poetry.
Shiny black metal and bright silver chrome,
Harleys and hardons.
They're all one and the same,
well-lubed sex machines, humming in the night.

I'm a natural-born sissy, I played jacks with my sisters.
I held a boy's hand during playground recess.
I dressed up for church, I always wore a bowtie.
I never let my shirt tails fall outside my chinos.
I wanted to be choirboy, to wear the pure white robes,
to walk in the processional, but that would never happen.

I liked board games, especially Go and Scrabble.
In junior high, I had my first crush on a boy.
I hid dirty magazines behind the bedroom bookcase.
Van Cliburn was my hero, I played our upright piano.
I didn't mind being a sissy, except for the bully Tom.
Camp was mostly boring, but I loved the leather shop.

I never dated girls or went to school dances.
I never kissed a girl, or wore her pretty dresses.
I always did my homework, I never once cheated.
I had a crush on Mr. Ness, who taught creative writing.
My Peter Max poster, put Barbra S. above my bed,
I never cared for team sports, I liked running solo.

My first wet dream was awesome, I was fourteen at the time.
I shot a load of cum, when I discovered my big boner.
It was thick and long, it felt a little heavy,
to touch the tip was heaven, it was slick and oily.
I was at it every night, with my jar of Vaseline,
shooting wads of creamy cum, out an open window.

In college a horny lover raped me on his kitchen floor.
Then he apologized, and kissed me head to toe.
I had a string of crushes, then I finally met up with Jim.
We moved to NYC, where I bought my leather jacket.
I wore it everywhere, it was like my second skin,
even during rush hour, in a noisy subway tearoom.

My first time in Hellfire, I watched two guys go at it.
One was dressed as a policeman. It was just a big charade.
A sex club in Chelsea had go-go boys on top of boxes.
I met my future husband in a biker's leather bar.
Abbey's super butch, but he's a softie deep inside.
Does that mean he's a sissy? It's no big deal either way.

23 - Otis, Jim and Joe

Oh, he may be weary,
Them young boys, they do get wearied,
wearing the same old shabby jeans.
But when he gets weary,
try a little tenderness.
Squeeze him, don't tease him, never ever leave him.

You know he's waiting,
Just anticipating,
the thing that you'll never possess.
Who will show him kindness?
Who will share his dreams?
try a little tenderness.

You are so beautiful to me. Can't you see?
You're everything I hoped for.
You're everything I need. You are so beautiful to me.
Longing in anticipation, hoping for a first touch.
So harmless, yet so thrilling. Do I dare to kiss him?
Squeeze him, don't tease him, never ever leave him.

I spill my seed for him.
When will you let my love in?
The time to hesitate is through,
no time to wallow in the mire,
come on baby, light my fire,
try to set the night on fire.

Once I finally got properly fucked,
our love took off. The dam broke.
Here comes the cock. Get it up.
Stay on the scene man. Like a sex machine.
We were making up for lost time,
with my well-lubed sex machine. Right on.

You're everything I hoped for.
You're the lover of my dreams.
You're everything I need.
You are so beautiful to me. Right on. Get it up.
Stay on the scene man. Like sex machine. Right on. Get it up.
We couldn't get much higher. Higher and higher.

24 - One Hundred Kisses

It's a hundred kisses, my head's in the clouds,
I see you clearly, even though it's still dark.
My heart is bursting, overflowing with love.
May I adore you? Kiss your warm darling ears?
They belong together, keeping track of the whispers,
of how much I love you, of how much I care.

It's a hundred kisses, my lips kiss your backside,
your skin is salty, like warm buttered toast.
You ask me to rub you, as you drift off to sleep,
the smell of your hair, leaves my cock so alive.
I fuss with your curls, I plant a kiss on your head,
I lick the back of your neck, then I kiss you again.

It's a hundred kisses, my hands caress your sweet butt,
it's soft and tender, I rim the deep crack.
I squeeze the cheeks firmly, feel their warmth with both hands,
my slaps pop loudly, your butt craves the burn.
I mount you gently, I'm lost in a dream,
I'm deep inside you, we're one in desire.

It's a hundred kisses, you're asleep on your back,
your chest is soft, familiar and warm.
Your nipples are red, hard as alabaster,
I bite them gently, you moan in deep bliss.
My tongue licks your tummy, I take hold of your cock,
it's already aroused, it's oily and wet.

It's a hundred kisses, I adore the hard shaft,
your beautiful sex organ, so proud and erect.
The balls hang heavy, so soft in my mouth,
the cockhead's perfect, the valley is fine.
I lick the crisp ridge, adore it all round,
you give me your seed, I savor each drop.

It's a hundred kisses, your eyes are my ocean,
lips soft and luscious, your tongue slippery and wet.
So completely erotic, I'm left dizzy and drunk,
I lick your beard stubble, your soft thick moustache.
I cherish your smile, once a shy boy's secret,
now his lover's treasure, worth a hundred more kisses.

25 ~ Paradise

At twilight, the elders tend to the garden,
collecting yellow leaves one by one.
Their bare feet sink into the soft moss,
as they carry their straw baskets.
The moss is moist and cool,
the garden is still and quiet.

At sunrise, darling boys wonder in,
sleepy-eyed and yawning.
Since the dawn of time,
baby boys have come here to wrestle.
They pair off on the soft green moss,
playing games of make-believe strength.

Morning's fair youths splash in the ponds,
churning the still water green.
Laughing noisily, playing rough,
they stop, out winded at last.
Proudly, they pull out their stiffening cocks,
shooting warm seed to the heavens.

Afternoon's athletic lovers,
arrive for sessions of sex.
They soon lose all abandon,
and are completely covered in sweat.
They service their cocks slow and deliberate,
with all the queer positions of love.

Master arrives as the golden sun sets,
his Butt-Boy is quietly waiting.
Master slaps the Boy's soft cheeks,
sharp pops are heard up in heaven.
Boy savors the smoldering burn,
as Master lubes his soft anus.

At twilight, boys and men return,
the garden is theirs for the evening.
For rest and most-private pleasure,
if the moon stays bright and clear.
Boys and men, settle down to sleep,
home in their Garden of Eden.

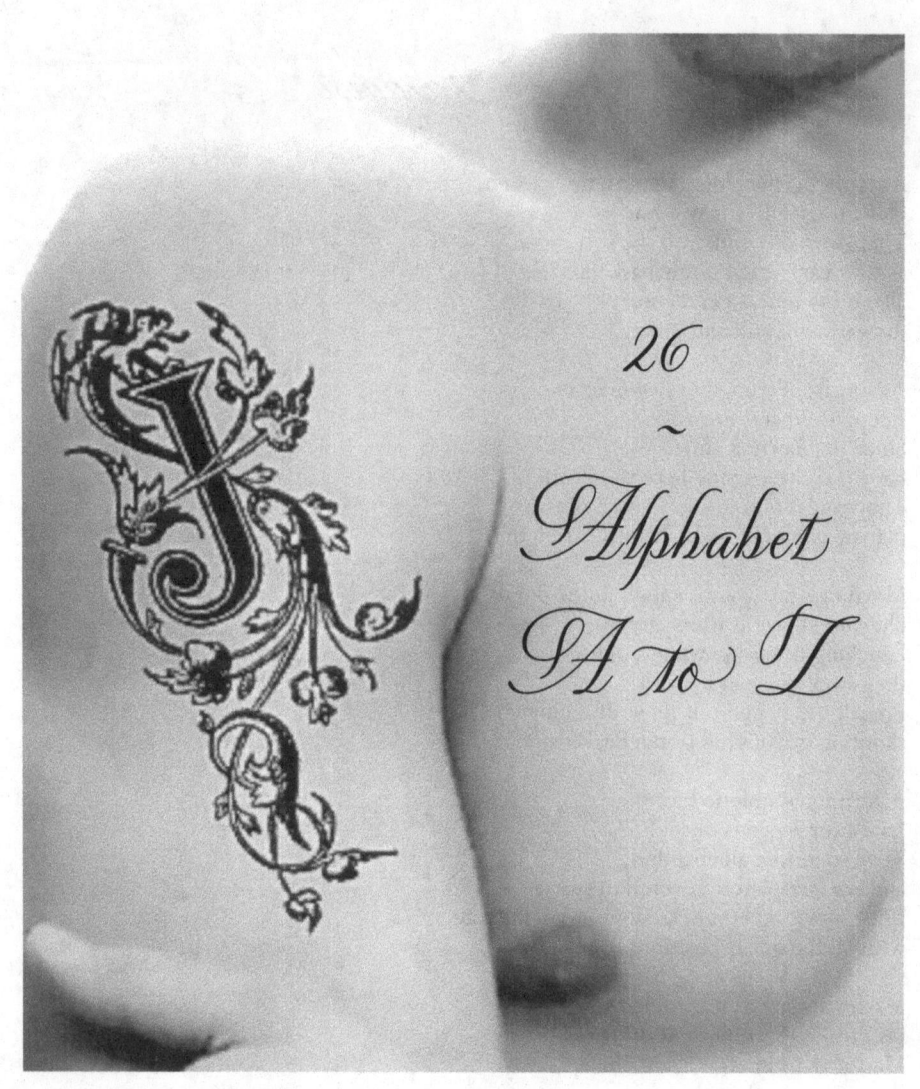

26
~
Alphabet
A to Z

A is for Abbey,
the love of my life.
God's sweetest creature,
he needn't a wife.

We're a couple of faggots,
made for each other.
Two peas in a pod,
Molly's the mother.

It's a family affair,
takes place in the city.
When Abbey met Miles,
he inherited his kitty.

From that day on,
they all lived together.
Never alone,
through all kinds of weather.

Molly hates thunder,
she hides under the bed.
Between the square pillows,
she has a soft spread.

Every night Molly,
checks out the bed.
She then settles in,
with her paw on my head.

$\mathcal{B}$ is for Bobby,
my first boyhood crush.
Hands joined at recess,
he made a boy blush.

Boys in the showers,
clowning around.
Bobby's the shy one,
he dares make no sound.

As Bobby grows older,
he opens his heart.
He learns to make love,
we never do part.

Bobby digs leather,
the jacket the chaps.
He never does drugs,
just poppers perhaps.

Bobby's an old man,
he still likes to screw.
He sleeps in my arms,
and prays in the pew.

Farewells at his graveside,
Bobby had AIDS.
A pile of dust,
a memory in spades.

C is for cock,
God's gift to mankind.
A boy's constant playmate,
his most precious find.

I'm off to Camp Oakley,
in the back of the bus.
When I showed them my weenie,
they made a big fuss.

Awake in our bunks,
we played every night.
Those queer horny boys,
were truly a sight.

Boys will be boys,
what can you say?
It's really harmless
like a roll in the hay.

Camp was terrific,
the guys were all hot.
It's all thanks to Sandy,
who stirred up the pot.

The kid was real cute,
he came from Louisiana.
He'd nap in my bunk,
and wear my bandana.

$\mathcal{D}$ is for drag queen,
with plenty of love.
Sequins and glitter,
blessed from above.

Men who play women,
no sissies are these.
First in at Stonewall,
while flaunting their heels.

They are the tough guys,
a match for the cops.
Breaking down doorways,
hurling big rocks.

Demanding our rights,
while making us proud.
The best of the best,
laughing out loud.

At the Invasion,
we welcomed you in.
Out came the big hugs,
we knew you were men.

We offered affection,
you wanted a snack.
You ladies were hot,
we showed you the Rack.

E is for envy,
I always crave more.
Hold on for dear life,
let's open the door.

As a young faggot,
I made the call.
How to shoot cum,
ten feet down the hall.

Later in school,
my buddies stroked meat.
We joined in a circle,
to make J.O. heat.

Subway tearoom,
you can hear the train.
Lookout at the doorway,
popper on the brain.

Meet up at the sex club,
things are really hot.
Check-in for the good stuff,
lube up on the spot.

Jack says he's finished,
but he craves one more.
What about the cute kid,
headed for the door?

$\mathscr{F}$ is for fucker,
my one and only dream.
Looking for some action,
letting off some steam.

In a station tearoom,
up against a wall.
The lad wants it rough,
while standing up tall.

He took it like a champ,
posing in his chaps.
Without the least resistance,
a bid at love perhaps.

Now it is my turn,
to show appreciation.
I turn the tables on him,
with an open invitation.

So we both took turns,
playing top and bottom.
Both were commonplace,
particularly at Sodom.

At the gate of heaven,
two men on the edge.
Desperate for true love,
let them make the pledge.

G is for Go Go,
a boy on a box.
Dancing his heart out,
as sly as a fox.

Bills in jock straps,
smiles on his face.
He's my Go Go Boy,
he naps at my place.

What a hot package,
tied up with a bow.
Open up his fly,
he'll put on a show.

Let them kiss your buttocks,
rub the sexy crack.
Slap your rosy butt cheeks,
then screw you in the sack.

My dear Go Go Boy
why are you so sad?
Let me kiss your forehead,
that can't feel so bad.

Back on top your box,
your ass is in the air.
A dozen crisp twenties,
falling from your hair.

H is for Heaven,
asleep in his arms.
Adrift on the ocean,
free of all harms.

Two bodies entwined,
united as one.
A single heartbeat,
the lone battle won.

Lovers forever,
safe on the seas.
A pair of queer sailors,
cocks out in the breeze.

Joined with our kisses,
tongues of desire.
Cock up our butts,
passions on fire.

One sailor's hammock,
shared by two queers.
Night after night,
free of all fears.

Bliss on the ocean,
men who love men.
Under the stars,
let's do it again.

$\mathscr{I}$ is for Initiation,
I'm long overdue.
Finally checking in,
a virgin plus a few.

It was called Le Club,
the check-in guy wore flowers.
He gave a welcome hug,
then sent me to the showers.

The lights were rosy red,
a sailor in the pool room.
The halls smelled vaguely musky,
a sweet kid in a costume.

He took me to the dungeon,
a level below ground.
It was kinda kinky,
I felt like I'd been bound.

By daybreak I emerged,
newest member of Le Club.
First of many evenings,
soaking in the tub.

Once initiated,
I blossomed like a queen.
Closer to my brothers,
could this be my scene?

J is for Junior,
the kid at the desk.
He's always so friendly,
is he looking for sex?

Junior is sweet,
he's always so polite.
Would he ever do us,
in the pool at night?

Junior surprised us,
he turned up the same night.
Footsies in the hot tub,
it was a pure delight.

Next morning at breakfast,
Junior served us buttered toast.
Our room key on the table,
a temptation for our host.

Ten minutes later,
a knock upon our door.
Junior is ready,
we all know the score.

Inside the shower,
we have a bit of fun.
Junior wants "full service,"
his pants are all undone.

$\mathcal{K}$ is for Kid,
the new guy in our gym.
He's a big mystery,
sexy and trim.

He spots me at the chest press,
his boner's in my face.
I have no complaints,
this guy's a super-ace.

His real name is Kevin,
but he prefers The Kid.
It makes him feel younger,
as if he's up for bid.

I'm three times his age,
but I must confess.
I look for him daily,
while we all undress.

Nice bod to look at,
in the pool for hours.
He hangs out in Speedos,
jerks off in the showers.

I don't know what to think,
could he just be gay?
I'll get him in the sack,
try some old foreplay.

L is for Lad,
dressed in pink for Easter,
He isn't a painter,
just a fashionesta.

The paint-splattered sneakers,
go with the broad brim hat.
He's a Sunday intellectual,
plus he owns the orange cat.

He just finished J.D. Salinger,
Catcher in the Rye.
Up next is Dostoevsky,
with C & P on the fly.

His hair is dirty blond,
his studied gate is slinky.
His favorite stone is jade,
he wears it on his pinky.

He's supposedly bi-sexual,
he'd fuck a total stranger.
A flower child at heart,
his idol's the Lone Ranger.

I suspect he's in the closet,
a tortured confused fag.
One day he may wake up,
and decide to turn to drag.

$\mathcal{M}$ is for Master,
Norman is his name.
Timmy is Norman's bottom
a slave would be the same.

Their S&M's an act,
the whip's pure fantasy.
It's all a fashion statement,
black leather happily.

Timmy prefers the paddle,
especially with a pop.
Norman digs the dildo,
he knows just when to stop.

Once they switched their sex roles,
it all went by much faster.
Neither knew what to do,
it was a disaster.

So they have routines,
favorites they both share.
Jerkoffs in the kitchen,
butt fucks on the stair.

Timmy is Norman's butt-boy,
sending him to heaven.
Norman is Timmy's deep-throat,
open seven to eleven.

$\mathcal{N}$ is for nudist,
Alex is his name.
He sheds his red bikini,
while playing any game.

Cards, tennis or charades,
Alex always strips down bare.
So he flaunts a big cock,
what does Alex care?

He only fucks the girls,
Alex is strictly straight.
He's sadly homophobic,
his cock's a loser's fate.

Once he answered the door,
with a full erection.
He forgot and let me in,
committing an indiscretion.

So he did me in the foyer,
tight up against a wall.
I felt his eight long inches,
so I stood up extra tall.

It's a shame he's such a hetero,
he really acts so gay.
What a sissy in his tight pants,
I'll jerk him off some day.

O is for Owen,
the New York City runner.
He's in his spandex shorts,
that show off his proud boner.

After laps around the Reservoir,
he always hits the Ramble.
That's where we meet up next,
for blowjobs nice and ample.

Owen is a champion,
he's won the golden ribbon.
He's one of the hard core,
about whom much is written.

I'm his greatest fan,
truly I am smitten.
I live to rub his butt,
as if he were my kitten.

After a hard run,
I lick his sweaty chest.
I kiss his rock hard abs,
then play his private guest.

Owen is my hero,
I gladly cheer him on.
He thinks he's James Bond,
that keeps him going strong.

$\mathcal{P}$is for Patrick,
my Catholic priest.
Dressed in his black robes,
he's ready to feast.

His smile is warm,
he's stuck on my crotch.
I'm fully aroused,
I'm ready to watch.

His blowjob is throaty,
he takes it down deep.
He's lost in the heavens,
without making a peep.

He takes my confession,
behind the red curtain.
A few Hail Mary's,
plus my cock, that's for certain.

The man has technique,
he's a true believer.
But he's still in the closet,
just another dreamer.

I'm back at his curtain,
each day for my fix.
A blowjob at noon,
at night a sweet mix.

Q is for queer,
a boy in a dress.
Pink satin undies,
no need to confess.

Queers proud of their cocks,
a new breed at last.
Demanding new rights,
just see to it fast.

It's a new world,
or is it the same?
Kids in the boondocks,
take most of the blame.

So you suck cock,
what's the big deal?
Try it sometime,
you might like the feel.

It started with nail polish,
a wig and high heels.
The dress was a breakthrough,
Drag shows make it real.

Some of us go butch,
we dig all our muscles.
Black leather you bet,
especially for couples.

$\mathscr{R}$ is for raw,
a new state of being.
Bold masculinity,
strong and unyielding.

Kurt ran the gym,
like a boot camp.
You better stop posing,
as if you're the champ.

It's really a family,
guys helping out.
Bullies aren't welcome,
it's your chance to come out.

Form must be perfect,
don't cheat on the reps.
Kurt misses nothing,
let's see your biceps.

I work on my six-pack,
It's starting to show.
Kurt says enough,
turn the focus below.

The guys are so friendly,
cheering me on.
Off to the steam room,
I'm getting turned on.

$\mathcal{S}$ is for sexy,
the new boy in town.
The smile of an actor,
and never a frown.

He's built like Adonis,
his shirt's never open.
He's terribly private,
he's always unspoken.

The guy's super shy,
as he enters a room.
He'd never do drag,
or so I assume.

He turned up at the tearoom,
but didn't go in.
He asked me to coffee,
which made my head spin.

Now was my big chance,
I kissed his soft cheek.
He gave me a hug,
then he started to weep.

After that noon tryst,
we're always a pair.
The best boy in town,
he's so debonair.

$\mathcal{T}$ is for Tex,
a drugstore cowboy.
He never rides horses,
that's just an old ploy.

Tex is a hustler,
on Christopher Street.
Always open for business,
never misses a beat.

Not once in a saddle,
it's all a big act.
He's skilled as a lover,
that's a matter of fact.

Ladies seek out his kisses,
gays pine for his butt.
Tex is totally flexible,
just show him the bucks.

He struts down the street,
red bandana in tow.
He portends a full basket,
ripe and ready to hoe.

Cock is his business,
but he'll settle for less.
A big pussycat,
Tex needs to confess.

$\mathcal{U}$ is for Unch,
classmate at Cornell.
My first gay buddy,
he was totally swell.

He came out before me,
hanging out in the bars.
Plus a steamy tearoom,
like landing on Mars.

I tagged along,
taking my time.
Unch never pushed me,
he never did crime.

Picnics with the orange Porsche,
on the Cornell Plantations.
Kisses on the grass,
less the orations.

Platonic boyfriends,
we hardly touched cock.
I slept in his arms.
until twelve o'clock.

Unch was my best friend,
My first secret lover.
He gave me my pride,
I owe him forever.

V is for varsity,
we played for the Pines.
Beach volleyball,
in our Speedos divine.

At the edge of the ocean,
we set up the net.
A dozen prissy queens,
not one willing to bet.

Bikinis and baseball caps,
were all that we needed.
Cheers from the fans,
were heartily greeted.

I was so proud,
Abbey scored the win.
The crowd went crazy,
they let out a din.

It's just a game,
faggots like to play.
Showing off our gym bods.
being extra gay.

When night came around,
the teams hit the sack.
More than a few,
met up in the Rack.

𝒲 is for wonder,
queers who are fine.
They know how to make love,
they're always divine.

Sometimes they're cranky,
impossible to please.
Usually they're sweethearts,
adorable with sleaze.

The young one's are well hung,
the old ones have money.
The ones in the middle,
are still looking for honey.

Time covers the bases,
Nothing is new.
Hustlers are human,
I've known quite a few.

Loneliness sucks,
we deserve more.
Let me buy you a drink,
please hold on the door.

Midnight in the Meat Rack,
Mr. Wonder appears.
He's as pure as an angel,
without any fears.

$\mathcal{X}$ is for ratings,
my favorite has three.
I have to admit,
I like what I see.

I put on some porno,
the kid's really cute.
But does he know opera?
Donizetti to boot.

I love the porn star,
Wagner can wait.
I dig the kid's style,
plus he's hot for a date.

Remember the old days,
when guys did it in trucks?
Now we meet on flat screens,
unsure if he fucks.

What happened to dining in,
or sending a poem?
I guess I'm old fashion,
I enjoy the unknown.

I still like my porno,
it's all triple X.
Some things never change,
an X is an X.

$\mathcal{Y}$ is for youth,
impatient and fine.
Horny as hell,
but truly divine.

Beautiful boys,
two kids on fire.
Searching for love,
rock hard with desire.

New feelings to process,
demands to be met.
Moments to cherish,
the sheets are all wet.

Beautiful glans,
a lad's perfect head.
The shaft is so regal,
not ready for bed.

Sex on the brain,
twenty-four seven.
Time for a reset,
praying to heaven.

What comes next,
a fat sugar daddy?
I don't think so,
I'll always love Abbey.

Z is for zap,
a slap on the ass.
A burning sensation,
I'll take a pass.

Hold on a minute,
don't move so fast.
I'll take another,
and please make it last.

I like the sound,
the sharp loud pop.
Give me another,
don't ever stop.

My butt's turning red,
get out the paddle.
I like your technique,
it's ripe for the saddle.

Cowboys can dig it,
I can see why.
Their chaps are so hot,
I'm eager to try.

So I'm all set,
ready to fuck,
Give me a zap,
I must be in luck.

www.ingramcontent.com/pod-product-compliance
Lightning Source LLC
Chambersburg PA
CBHW011924060726
47496CB00012BA/3023